HERB CAEN was probably one of America's best-known local columnists. A native of Sacramento, he began his newspaper career there before moving to San Francisco in 1936. His witty, humorous, and often acid column, which appeared every day in the San Francisco *Chronicle*, became a West Coast institution. Though he published such successful adult books as *Don't Call It Frisco*, *Baghdad by the Bay* and *Only in San Francisco*, THE CABLE CAR AND THE DRAGON marked his debut as a children's book author.

BARBARA NINDE BYFIELD was born in Abilene, Texas. She has illustrated several children's books, including *Upright Hilda*, *The Giant Sandwich*, and *The Mystery of the Spanish Silver Mine*, and is the author-illustrator of *The Eating in Bed Cookbook*, *The Glass Harmonica*, and *The Haunted Spy*. Mrs. Bayfield lives with her two daughters in New York City.

D0573121

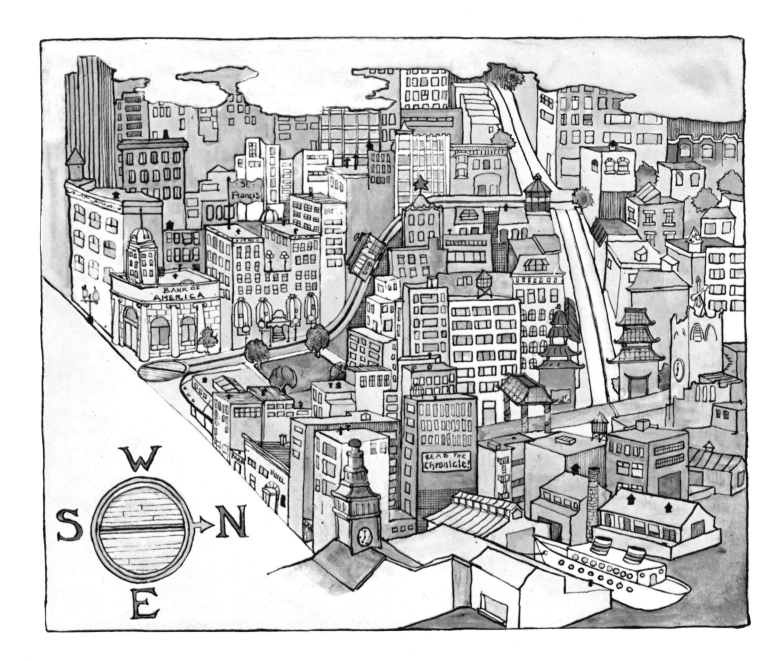

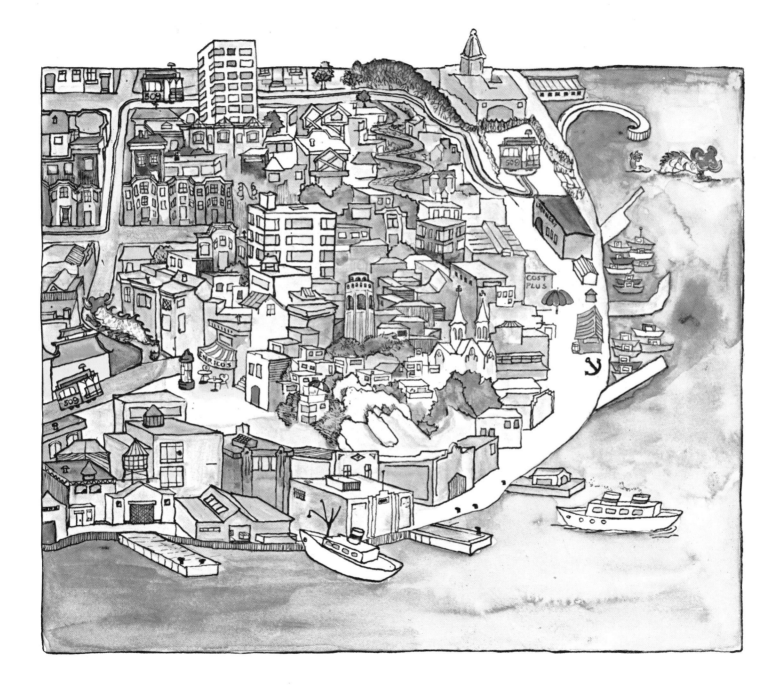

THE CABLE CAR AND THE DRAGON

by HERB CAEN

Illustrated by

BARBARA NINDE BYFIELD

THE CABLE CAR
AND THE DRAGON

chronicle books·san francisco

Manufactured in China, in April 2012

Library of Congress Cataloging-in-Publication Data

Caen, Herb, 1916 – 1997
  The cable car and the dragon.

  Summary: Tired of traveling the same route, a San Francisco
cable car takes a different turn and ends up in Chinatown during
New Year's celebrations.
  ISBN-13: 978-0-8118-1054-8
  ISBN-10: 0-8118-1054-2
  [1. Cable cars—Fiction. 2. San Francisco (Calif.)—Fiction]
I. Byfield, Barbara Ninde, ill. II. Title.
  PZ7.C1175Cab   1986   [E]   85-32004
  793.73—dc20

Published by arrangement with Doubleday & Company, Inc.

This product conforms to CPSIA 2008.

10 9 8 7

Chronicle Books LLC
680 Second Street
San Francisco, California 94107

www.chroniclekids.com

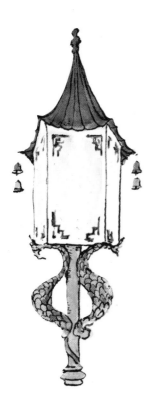

For my son, Christopher, who, having had the taste and judgment to be born in San Francisco in 1965, knows quite a bit about cable cars and dragons. He also knows enough about his father to listen to the following tale with an air of polite disbelief.

His name is Charlie and he's sixty years old. That may sound very old to you, but it's not old for a cable car. In fact, Charlie is the youngest cable car in San-Francisco, where he and I both live. All the other cable cars in San Francisco are about a hundred years old, and they are so old and rickety you wonder how they manage to get around at all.

I ride on Charlie's back almost every day—along with a lot of other people. We climb on downtown at Powell and Market streets, and then off we go up the steep hills and down into the valleys, all the way to San Francisco Bay.

Boy, is it an exciting ride! We go past big buildings and little ones, new ones and old, through the parts where the Chinese and the Italians live. The last part is the best. We come to a great big hill called Russian Hill—nobody knows how it got that name—and then we slide down to the bottom, just like a roller coaster, to the Bay.

Just when you think you're going to go right into the water, the cable car suddenly turns into a pretty little park, and that's the end of the line. It's about the best ride in the world.

In the old days, when horses were the only way to get around, besides walking, those hills were really a problem. The horses had to pull streetcars up the hills.

And they had to pull carriages, which were like automobiles without motors, and big trucks that carried groceries and laundry and furniture.

On rainy days sometimes the poor horses would slip on the hills and break their legs. Other horses would die at an early age from working too hard. The streets were covered with big stones to help the horses get a toe-hold, but it was still hard on them.

Some people even said, "Why not just tear down the hills and make this a flat city?" But if they'd done that, San Francisco wouldn't have been San Francisco. It's the hills, with their wonderful view of the Bay and the countryside, that make San Francisco different from other cities.

It was just about then, with the horses having such a hard time, that a Scotsman named Andrew Hallidie arrived in San Francisco. Oh, it was a great day for the city! For in 1873, he invented the cable car. His idea was so simple that nobody had ever thought of it before.

"What we'll do," he said, "is run ropes of steel under the hills. They'll all be attached to a big motor that goes around and around. Then my little cars will hold onto the cables and be pulled up the hills and slide down the other side."

Of course there were a lot of people who said it couldn't be done. There always are. But one day Mr. Hallidie strung a cable up the Clay Street hill, which is very

steep, and showed San Francisco that it COULD be done. The little car grabbed onto the cable with its metal hand and went shooting up the hill, as thousands cheered.

At the top, the little cable car reached up with its other hand and gave the bell a triumphant ring: "Ding-ding-a-ding-ding DING DING!" Some of the people said, "Why that little car is almost human!"

They didn't know it then, but they were right. Cable cars are so human they can even speak. One of them can, anyway.

San Francisco, with all that water around it, is very windy. And sticking out into the ocean that way, it is also foggy. When the city is all covered with fog, it's like living inside a great gray pearl.

It was on such a night that I found I could talk to Charlie the Cable Car. It was so foggy that you couldn't even see the tops of the buildings. And so windy that all the tourists had gone to bed early.

Charlie was sitting forlornly on the wooden turntable at Powell and Market streets, waiting to be turned around so he could start up the hill again. There wasn't another person in sight when I climbed aboard and sat on his bench at the front. I knew it was Charlie because I'd let him carry me so many times. Sometimes, in fact, I'd wait for him because, as I've already told you, he was only sixty—the youngest of the cable cars—and he could climb the hills a lot faster than the others.

Since there weren't any other people around, I thought I'd find out if he'd talk to me.

"Hello, Charlie," I said.

"Hello there," he said in a grumpy voice. He sounded just as I thought he would —like a piece of wood being rubbed across steel.

"Pardon me if I sound tired," he went on, "but it has been a tough day. I'm only supposed to carry forty people—that's the law, you know—and there must have been a hundred people on every trip, half of them hanging onto my sides. Sometimes I feel like quitting."

"Oh, don't do that," I said hastily. "You're the very best cable car in San Francisco. In fact, I'd like to shake your hand."

"Okay," he shrugged, pulling his right hand out of the cable slot and gripping mine.

"Ouch!" I cried. "You sure have a strong grip. Uh—like steel!"

He chuckled at that. Then he added, "I probably got grease all over your hand, but I can't help it." I nodded, wiping my hand on my handkerchief.

"Anyway," he said in a kinder rasp, "I'm glad to see you. I hate to make my last trip of the night all alone. Well, turn me around and let us be off."

After I had swung him around on the wooden turntable, he stuck his right

hand back down into the slot and grabbed onto the cable. With his left hand, he reached up and rang the bell: "Ding-ding-a-ding-ding DING DING!" And off we went toward the first big hill, called Nob Hill, almost invisible in the fog.

Charlie was breathing a little heavily as we got to the top of Nob Hill. "Sometimes," he panted, "I think I'm getting a little old for this job. Every year this hill seems to get steeper and steeper."

"Nonsense," I said, patting him on the back. "Just remember that San Francisco wouldn't be the same without you. Besides, you're FAMOUS. Every day the tourists take thousands of pictures of you with their cameras. I'll bet you've had your picture taken more times than a movie star."

"Maybe so," Charlie answered. "But I'm not having any FUN. I run along the same old streets every day. Think about it. For sixty years, I've been going up and down these hills, stuck on these tracks, hanging onto that cable for dear life. Shucks, I don't even know what the rest of San Francisco looks like."

I didn't know what to say to that. Charlie always looked to me like a happy cable car, but now I could see I was wrong. Poor Charlie.

As we passed the top of Nob Hill, we could look down into Chinatown, on our right. It was ablaze with lights. Bands were playing. There seemed to be thousands of people in the narrow streets.

"What's going on down there?" grumbled Charlie.

"It's Chinese New Year's," I replied. "You know, the Chinese have a different New Year than we do. It comes in February or March, depending on where the moon is. They shoot off firecrackers, to scare away the evil spirits. They give each other presents, wrapped in red paper, because red means good luck. And right now they're having their New Year's parade, led by the biggest dragon you ever saw."

"A DRAGON!" gasped Charlie. Then he stamped his steel foot on the steel rail, shooting out great sparks. "Now that's exactly what I've been talking about. I've been running up and down San Francisco for sixty years, and I have NEVER seen a Chinese New Year's parade OR a Chinese dragon!"

Muttering to himself, we moved slowly across the top of Nob Hill to Jackson Street, where he was supposed to turn left toward Russian Hill. But instead of turning, he stopped suddenly.

"I'm not turning left tonight," he shouted, his headlight flaring up in the fog. "Tonight, for the first time in my life, I am turning RIGHT! I just have to see that Chinese dragon!"

"But, Charlie," I pleaded. "You can't do that. In the first place, there aren't any tracks to Chinatown. And in the second place, if your boss finds out, you'll lose your job."

"My boss!" snorted Charlie. "He's home asleep, and anyway I don't care. I'm going to Chinatown and that's THAT. It's time *I* had a little fun."

Well, there was nothing I could do to stop him. Slowly and clumsily, he pulled himself off the tracks, first letting go of the cable. "That feels better already," he smiled, rubbing his metal hands together.

We started slowly down the Jackson Street hill toward Chinatown. Charlie's wheels were cutting big holes in the pavement, and he had a hard time walking.

"Boy," he said, "my feet are killing me already. I guess I've been traveling on rails too long. But don't worry, I'll make it."

He paused at the edge of Grant Avenue, Chinatown's main street, and looked at the huge crowd. "You know," he said slowly, "this is the most exciting thing that has happened to me since I lost my grip on Russian Hill— and THAT was fifty years ago!"

He looked at me suspiciously. "Say," he snapped. "You're not going to tell anybody about this, are you? I mean, I wouldn't want people to think I went off my trolley."

"No, Charlie," I assured him. "It's our secret. Now that we're here, I want you to have a good time."

"That's the spirit!" he whooped, ringing his bell and pushing his way through

the crowd. At last we got to the corner where the parade was beginning and there we saw the great Chinese dragon.

"Good heavens, he looks fierce!" gasped Charlie. And so he did. The dragon's head was almost as wide as the street—all gold and red, with dozens of bells in the top, shaking and ringing. His eyes were big as saucers, black and angry, red in the center. A long pink tongue flicked out from between his shining white teeth, and he breathed real fire! As for his body, it was a block long—all covered with scales, like a silvery fish—and his pointed tail swished back and forth.

"Let's get out of here," cried Charlie, frightened at the sight. "Let's get back on the tracks where it's safe."

"No turning back now," I said. "Besides," I went on, not meaning a word of it, "he's probably not as mean as he looks." Shivering just a little, I walked up to the monster's head and grinned weakly, "Happy New Year, Mr. Dragon!"

"My name isn't Mr. Dragon," he replied in a surprisingly pleasant voice, shooting out a flame six feet long. "Sorry about that," he added hastily. "I only flame when I talk. Can't help it, you know. Dragons are built that way. Anyway, my name isn't Mr. Dragon, it's Chu Chin Chow, but you may call me Chu. I'm very much obliged to you for wishing me a Happy New Year. You're the first person who has been thoughtful enough to do THAT."

"You speak very well—er—for a Chinese dragon," I said.

"Naturally," he replied, his flame setting fire to my shoelaces. "Stand to one side. I can only flame straight ahead. I speak good English because I've been in this country sixty years. When I'm not in this parade, I live up in the hills, out of sight of everybody, and what a bore THAT is. Say, who's your funny-looking friend?"

I was delighted. "This is Charlie the Cable Car," I said, beaming, "and you two have a lot to talk about. He's just as old as you are. And he hasn't been having any fun, either. Besides, you're the first Chinese dragon he has ever seen."

"Now isn't that a coincidence!" smiled Chu, looking nice as pie. "Charlie, you're the first cable car I'VE ever seen! I've heard about you guys all my life."

"Pleased to meet you, Chu," said Charlie, extending his grip and pulling it back suddenly as Chu smiled a super flame.

"Tell you what, Charlie," whispered the dragon in a very confidential tone, "I want you to be my guest in the parade. You can get under the end of my tail, where nobody can see you. And then—.

Chu waggled his huge head this way and that to make sure nobody was listening. "And then," he went on, "when the parade is over, I'm going to do exactly what YOU did. I'm going to sneak away and take a ride with you—yes I am! Why, I've ALWAYS wanted to ride on a San Francisco cable car!"

"Put 'er there, friend," laughed Charlie, sticking out his grip again. And getting it burned again.

A few minutes later, the parade began amid an ear-splitting burst of firecrackers. As usual, it was a great success. Chu growled fiercely at the thousands of people, making the children scream with horrified delight. Some of the naughtier ones would try to grab Chu's tail, but every time they did, Charlie would frighten them away by ringing his bell loudly and stamping his steel feet.

Some of the old-timers kept saying, "Hey, aren't those WHEELS under the dragon's tail?" But, fortunately, with all the screaming and all the firecrackers, nobody heard them.

And when the naughty children cried, "That old dragon has a cable car bell in his tail!" their parents said, "Stop making up such silly stories."

At the end of Grant Avenue, where there were hardly any people, Chu swung his head around toward his tail and called out, "*Psst,* Charlie, let's go. And thanks for scaring off those mean little kids. You know, my tail is very tender, and it's the only part of me I can't protect. I really appreciate what you did!"

When they were sure nobody was looking, the cable car and the dragon began scrambling up a dark side street, with me puffing along in the rear. Back on Powell Street, almost invisible in the fog, Charlie slid himself back onto his tracks, murmur-

ing "Ahhhh, that feels better. My poor feet!" He reached his right hand down into the slot and grabbed the cable. With his left hand, he reached up and rang the bell: "Ding-ding-a-ding-ding DING DING!"

"Come on, Chu!" he whooped. "All aboard!"

The great dragon, his twenty feet scratching and scuffling, slithered onto the cable car, and I squeezed onto a seat alongside him. "Boy, this is the life," he roared, crossing his twenty legs. Reaching between the scales on his chest, he pulled out a big black cigar and popped it into his mouth.

"Here," I said, reaching into my jacket, "let me light that for you."

"No need," he grinned, darting a small flame out of his mouth and setting fire to the end of the cigar. "Charlie," he went on as we began rolling along, "this is the most exciting night of my life—I'm finally getting a ride on a cable car!"

When we reached the top of Russian Hill, Charlie paused to catch his breath.

"You know, Chu," he said, puffing and panting like a steam engine, "you are one heavy dragon. I don't want to hurt your feelings, but you're the biggest load I've ever carried." Groaning, he added, "Oh, my achin' back!"

Just then a fog horn in the Bay went "EEEeeee-ohhhhh."

"That's exactly the way I feel," sighed Charlie. "Well, let's go. One last hill and I'm through for the night. Hang on!"

We started down the long, steep slope to the busy street at the bottom, Charlie gripping the cable and ringing his bell as loud as he could. Half way down, he was going so fast that I hollered, "Hey, is anything wrong?" Chu nervously threw his cigar away. "Wow!" he said, his eyes like two big searchlights and his breath coming in short darts of flame.

"I th-think I lost my grip," gasped Charlie, plunging his right arm deeper into the slot. He jammed on his wooden brakes and there was a smell of burning wood. "Brakes aren't holding!" he yelled.

Now we were skidding and sliding toward the automobiles crossing the street at the bottom of the hill. "Still can't find the cable," yelled Charlie in a panic. "We're running away!"

I closed my eyes and hung on for dear life. I feared the very worst. Either Charlie would run into an automobile, or, if we missed a car by some miracle, we would plunge into the Bay.

But there WAS a miracle, and it was Chu Chin Chow who did it. With surprising speed, the great dragon slid off the cable car. As it raced past, his huge tail lashed out and coiled itself around Charlie's rear platform. Then, roaring and spitting flames a foot long, Chu braced his twenty powerful legs against the hill. His big claws dug into the street, tearing up the pavement. But slowly, oh so slowly, Charlie came to a halt—just a few yards short of the busy street.

Chu crouched on the tracks, absolutely worn out.

"Thanks, Chu," said Charlie in a weak voice. "I thought we were all goners, for sure." He mopped his wet windshield with a shaking hand, and then fished down into the slot. "Ah, there's the cable. Get back on, and I'll ride you to the end of the line."

"Let's wait a minute until all the cars pass," said Chu. "I don't want anybody to see me outside of Chinatown—I just hate to frighten people if I don't have to, you

know." He paused and looked surprised. "Hey! I worked so hard I blew out my flame!"

Turning to me, he asked, "Please light your lighter and hold it in front of my mouth." I did, and the dragon breathed "*Ahhhhhhhh.*" There was a rumbling sound from deep inside him and his flame sprang to life. "THAT's better," he nodded.

At the end of the line, Charlie, Chu, and I all shook hands.

"You know, Chu, you saved our lives," said Charlie, "and I'll never forget you."

"Think nothing of it," replied Chu lightly. "You saved my tail from getting hurt in Chinatown, so we're even. Well, it's back to the country for me. It was a great ride, but I wouldn't want to try it again!"

With that, the great dragon slid into the dark Bay and began swimming toward the distant hills. "Happy New Year!" we called out. He turned his beautiful golden head and shot out one long flame. Then he was gone from our lives.

HERB CAEN was probably one of America's best-known local columnists. A native of Sacramento, he began his newspaper career there before moving to San Francisco in 1936. His witty, humorous, and often acid column, which appeared every day in the San Francisco *Chronicle*, became a West Coast institution. Though he published such successful adult books as *Don't Call It Frisco*, *Baghdad by the Bay* and *Only in San Francisco*, THE CABLE CAR AND THE DRAGON marked his debut as a children's book author.

BARBARA NINDE BYFIELD was born in Abilene, Texas. She has illustrated several children's books, including *Upright Hilda*, *The Giant Sandwich*, and *The Mystery of the Spanish Silver Mine*, and is the author-illustrator of *The Eating in Bed Cookbook*, *The Glass Harmonica*, and *The Haunted Spy*. Mrs. Bayfield lives with her two daughters in New York City.

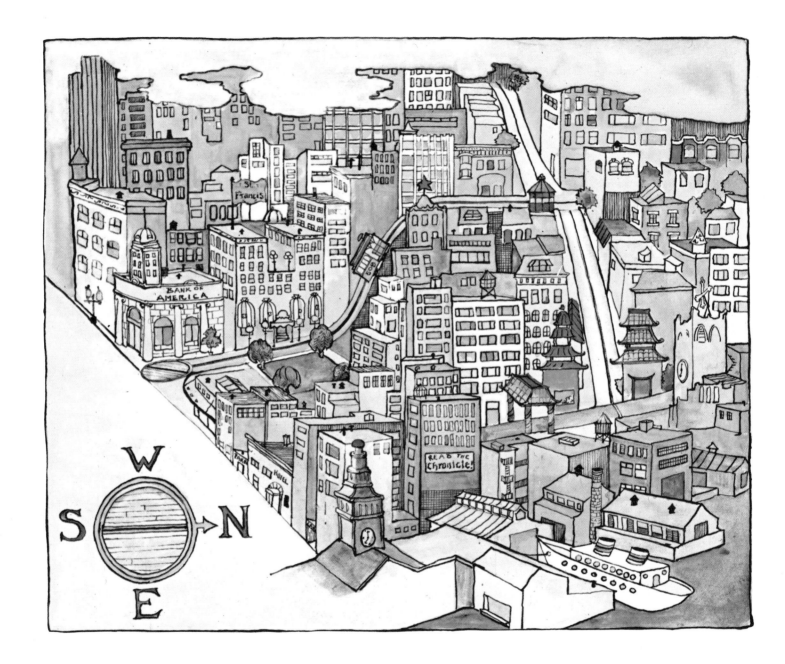

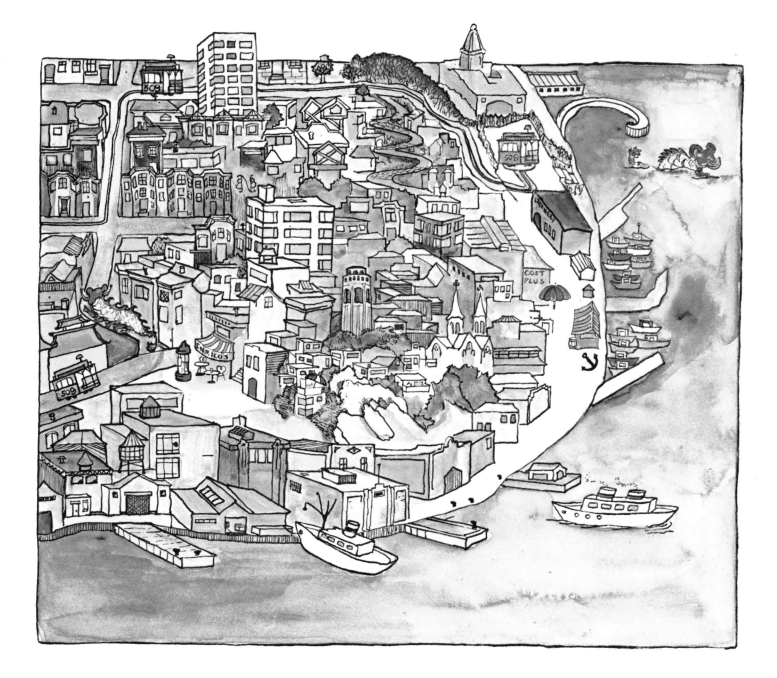

This is the rollicking tale of the adventures of Charlie, the youngest cable car.
Only sixty years old, he is tired of the same old rut.
One night as he's puffing himself up Nob Hill, he hears a lot of excitement
down below: Chinese New Year! Suddenly, Charlie take a right turn at
Jackson Street, rather than the left he has taken for sixty years,
and he finds himself in the middle of the parade.
There he meets a friendly dragon named Chu Chin Chow,
who is also bored with his job. Charlie treats Chu to a cable car
ride that looks as if it will end in a disastrous plunge into
the San Francisco Bay—unless a miracle occurs.